nickelodeon™

Dora & Diego

DORA AND DIEGO'S TREASURE HUNT

adapted by Leslie Valdes

based on the screenplay
written by Chris Gifford

illustrated by Dave Aikins

Simon Spotlight/Nickelodeon
New York   London   Toronto   Sydney

y published as
rate Adventure

Based on the TV series *Dora the Explorer*™ as seen on Nick Jr.™

SIMON SPOTLIGHT/NICKELODEON
An imprint of Simon & Schuster Children's Publishing Division
1230 Avenue of the Americas, New York, New York 10020
© 2005 Viacom International Inc. All rights reserved. NICKELODEON, NICK JR.,
Dora the Explorer, and all related titles, logos, and characters are registered trademarks of Viacom International Inc.
All rights reserved, including the right of reproduction in whole or in part in any form.
SIMON SPOTLIGHT and colophon are registered trademarks of Simon & Schuster, Inc.
For information about special discounts for bulk purchases, please contact Simon & Schuster Special Sales
at 1-866-506-1949 or business@simonandschuster.com.
Manufactured in the United States of America 1210 LAK
This Simon Spotlight edition 2011
2 4 6 8 10 9 7 5 3 1
ISBN 978-1-4424-1391-7
Previously published as *Dora's Pirate Adventure*

Ahoy, mateys! I'm Dora. Do you want to be in our pirate play? Great! Let's go put on our costumes!

Uh-oh. That sounds like pirates. Do you see pirates?

The Pirate Piggies are taking our costume chest! They think it's full of treasure.

If we don't get the costumes back, we can't dress up like pirates. And if we can't dress up like pirates, then we can't put on our pirate play.

We can get our costumes back. We just have to know where to go. Who do we ask for help when we don't know where to go? The Map!

Map says the Pirate Piggies took the treasure chest to Treasure Island. We have to sail across the Seven Seas and go under the Singing Bridge, and that's how we'll get to Treasure Island.

Do you see the Seven Seas? Yeah, there they are!
We can use that boat to sail across!

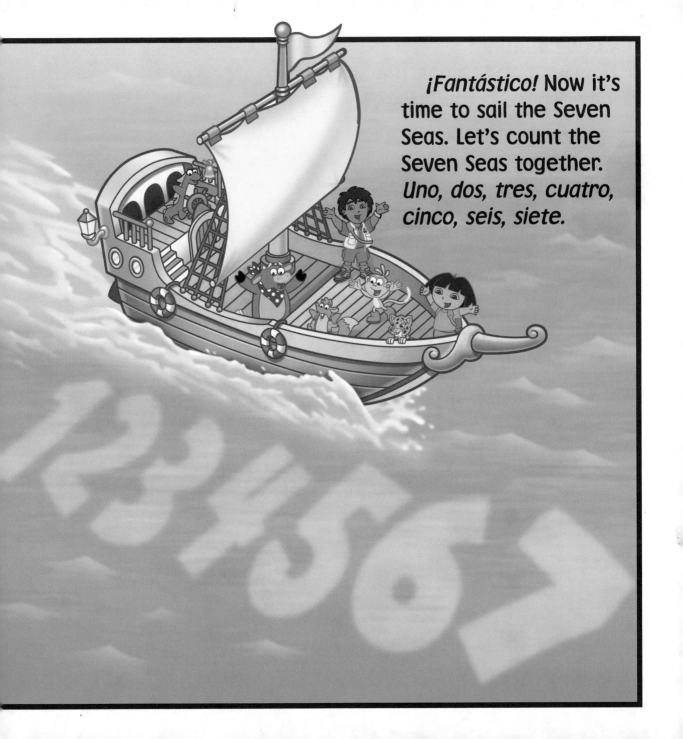

¡Fantástico! Now it's time to sail the Seven Seas. Let's count the Seven Seas together. *Uno, dos, tres, cuatro, cinco, seis, siete.*

Good counting!
Now we need to find the Singing Bridge. Where is the bridge?

Yeah, there it is. *¡Vámonos!*

We have to teach him the right words.
Let's sing the song the right way.

Row, row, row your boat,
Gently down the stream,
Merrily, merrily, merrily, merrily,
Life is but a dream!

Yay! We made it past the Singing Bridge! Next up is Treasure Island. Do you see Treasure Island? Yeah, there it is!

Look! There's a waterfall. Isa has to turn the wheel, or we'll go over the edge.

Uh-oh! The wheel broke! Maybe Backpack has something that will help us. Quick, say "Backpack!"

We need something to fix the wheel. Do you see the sticky tape?
Yeah, there it is! *¡Muy bien!*

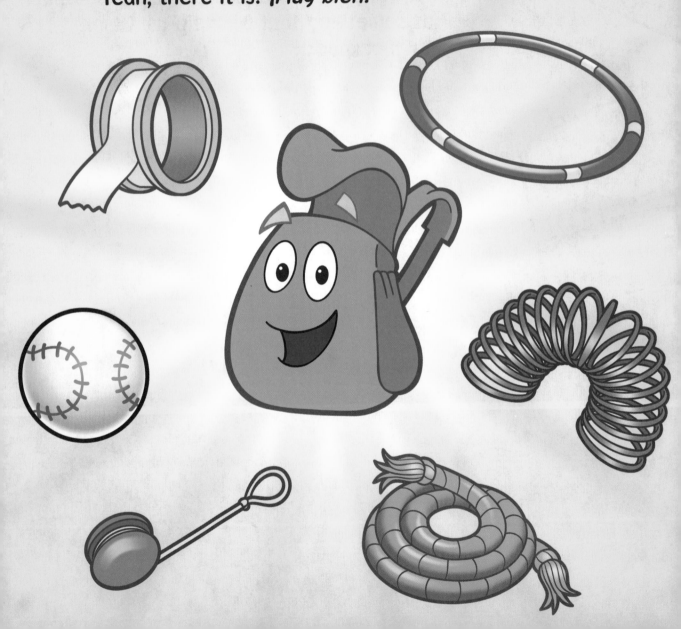

Turn the wheel, Isa!
Whew! We made it past the waterfall.
Come on! Let's go to Treasure Island, and get our costumes back!

We found Treasure Island. Now let's look for the treasure chest. We can use Diego's spotting scope.

There it is! Come on, mateys, let's go get our costumes back!

The Pirate Piggies say they won't give us back our treasure. We need your help. When I count to three, you need to say "Give us back our treasure!" Ready? One, two, three: Give us back our treasure!

It worked! *¡Muy bien!* The Pirate Piggies say we can have
our treasure chest back!

Thanks for helping us get our costumes back. Now we can put on our pirate play. We did it! Hooray!